Sealed With A Kiss

Look for more

titles:

#1 It's a Twin Thing
#2 How to Flunk Your First Date
#3 The Sleepover Secret
#4 One Twin Too Many
#5 To Snoop or Not to Snoop
#6 My Sister the Supermodel
#7 Two's a Crowd
#8 Let's Party
#9 Calling All Boys
#10 Winner Take All
#11 P.S. Wish You Were Here
#12 The Cool Club
#13 War of the Wardrobes
#14 Bye-Bye Boyfriend
#15 It's Snow Problem
#16 Likes Me, Likes Me Not
#17 Shore Thing
#18 Two for the Road
#19 Surprise, Surprise!

TWO of a kind™

Sealed With A Kiss

by Judy Katschke

from the series created by
Robert Griffard
& Howard Adler

A PARACHUTE PRESS BOOK

A PARACHUTE PRESS BOOK

Parachute Publishing, L.L.C.
156 Fifth Avenue, Suite 302
New York, NY 10010

Published by
HarperEntertainment
An Imprint of HarperCollins*Publishers*
10 East 53rd Street, New York, NY 10022-5299

TWO OF A KIND books created and produced by
Parachute Press, L.C.C., in cooperation with Dualstar Publications,
a division of Dualstar Entertainment Group, Inc.,
published by HarperEntertainment, an imprint of
HarperCollins Publishers.
Cover photograph courtesy of Dualstar Entertainment Group, Inc. ©2001

 TM & © Dualstar Entertainment Group, Inc., 2001

ISBN 0-06-106660-5

First printing: December 2001

Printed in the United States of America

Visit HarperEntertainment on the World Wide Web at
www.harpercollins.com

10 9 8 7 6 5

CHAPTER ONE

"We're going home to Chicago for only two weeks!" Mary-Kate Burke told her sister, Ashley. She grunted as she struggled to zip Ashley's duffel bag. "Why do you need all these clothes?"

Ashley sat on her duffel bag and bounced up and down.

"Fourteen days means fourteen outfits," she said. "And I want to be prepared for everything!"

It was Sunday, and winter break at the White Oak Academy for Girls had just started. That meant a break from classes, homework, and tests. And since White Oak was a boarding school in New Hampshire—it meant going home!

"Done," Mary-Kate said, zipping the last inch.

1

Exhausted, she flopped down on Phoebe Cahill's bed. Phoebe was Ashley's roommate. She had already left for San Francisco.

"Wait!" Ashley cried out. "I forgot to pack my bathing suit and flip-flops."

"Bathing suit?" Mary-Kate shrieked. "But the winters in Chicago are ice cold!"

"There are indoor pools," Ashley said.

Ashley flopped down next to Mary-Kate. "I can't believe we're going home tomorrow." She sighed.

Mary-Kate stared at the ceiling and smiled. She and Ashley loved boarding school. They had made great friends, joined cool clubs, and learned lots of neat stuff. But they still couldn't wait to go home.

"We're going to have a blast with Dad and our Chicago friends," Mary-Kate said excitedly. "Movies! Parties—"

"Rub it in, why don't you?" a girl's voice muttered.

The twins sat up. Mary-Kate saw their friends Elise Van Hook and Cheryl Miller standing in the doorway. They didn't look happy. And Mary-Kate knew why.

Cheryl and Elise were stuck at school for winter break. Cheryl's airline went on strike just after she bought her ticket. As for Elise, her parents were

Peace Corps volunteers in Fiji, a tropical island in the Pacific Ocean.

"Are you guys sure you can't go home?" Mary-Kate asked.

"Why can't you just get another flight, Cheryl?" Ashley asked.

"On what—Santa's sleigh?" Cheryl grumbled. "It's the holidays. All the flights are already booked."

"And my parents are busy working," Elise said. "But that's okay." She forced a smile. "Decorating palm trees with candy canes isn't my thing."

Mary-Kate felt bad. Even Elise's glitter eye shadow and lip gloss weren't enough to brighten her gloomy face.

"Think of us when you're in Chicago," Cheryl said sadly. "Sleeping in an abandoned dorm . . . "

"Eating eggnog oatmeal . . . " Elise added.

Mary-Kate shuddered. White Oak had a tradition of serving a different flavor of oatmeal every day. Eggnog was a definite possibility!

"I wish there were something we could do for them," Mary-Kate whispered as Elise and Cheryl turned to leave. "Staying in school over winter break must be the pits!"

"Yeah," Ashley whispered back. "If I had room in

3

my duffel bag I'd pack them in and bring them home with us."

That's when it clicked.

"What an awesome idea!" Mary-Kate cried. She ran to the door and called out into the hall, "Cheryl, Elise! Wait!"

Cheryl and Elise returned to the room.

"What's up?" Cheryl asked.

"Ashley and I just thought of a way to get you out of school for the holidays!" Mary-Kate said.

"You did?" Elise gasped.

"We did?" Ashley asked, confused.

"You are coming home with us!" Mary-Kate said.

"Hey, yeah!" Ashley said, grinning.

"Both of us?" Cheryl asked.

"All the way to Chicago?" Elise asked.

"Why not?" Ashley said. "Our dad was supposed to fly back from South America three days ago. He's probably driving to New Hampshire to pick us up right now."

The girls' dad, Kevin Burke, was a science professor. He often led student tours in the Amazon in South America. Last time he had his students studying exotic insects. This time—poisonous frogs!

"Oh, come on!" Mary-Kate urged. "Whoever heard of spending Christmas at school anyway?"

"Are you sure your dad won't mind?" Cheryl asked.

"Positive!" Mary-Kate said. "He's always saying the more the merrier. Especially on Christmas!"

"And Mary-Kate and I love having sleepover guests," Ashley said. "As long as they don't mess up my side of the room—or tidy up Mary-Kate's."

"Cute," Mary-Kate said with a smirk.

But Ashley had a point. For sisters, they were pretty different. Mary-Kate loved sports and drama. Ashley loved clothes, writing for the White Oak *Acorn*—and boys!

Ashley even had a boyfriend, Ross Lambert. He went to the Harrington School for Boys just a few miles down the road. Harrington and White Oak were brother-sister schools. That meant sharing classes, activities, and if you were lucky—a date!

"Well?" Ashley asked Cheryl and Elise.

Cheryl and Elise smiled at each other and shrugged.

"The thought of eggnog oatmeal is pretty depressing," Elise said.

"And I did always want to taste a real Chicago hot dog," Cheryl added.

"So the answer is yes?" Ashley asked.

"Of course it's yes!" Elise said.

5

"Cool!" Mary-Kate cried. They all began jumping up and down. "And wait until you see how they light up the Sears Tower for Christmas!"

"Do you think we can go to a Cubs game?" Elise asked, still jumping up and down.

"It's December, Elise," Cheryl said. "No baseball."

"Oh," Elise said. She tapped her head. "Du-uh!"

Mary-Kate couldn't wait. "I'm going to call Dad on his cell phone," she said. "And give him the great news."

Mary-Kate backed out of the room and almost bumped into Ms. Viola. Ms. Viola was the housemother for Porter House, their dorm.

"Mary-Kate and Ashley," Ms. Viola said. "There's a phone call from your dad down the hall."

"Dad?" Mary-Kate asked. "What a coincidence!"

"And when you're done," Ms. Viola went on, "Mrs. Pritchard wants to see all of you girls in her office."

"I wonder why," Mary-Kate said after Ms. Viola left.

"Probably to wish us a happy holiday," Ashley said.

Mrs. Pritchard was the White Oak headmistress—or the head, as everyone called her.

Everyone liked Mrs. Pritchard, even though she made them all wake up really early for morning announcements.

"Let's take Dad's call," Mary-Kate said. She turned to Cheryl and Elise. "We'll be back in a flash. In the meantime, start packing for the windy city."

"Yippeee!" Elise cheered.

The twins hurried down the hall. Porter House was practically empty. And so quiet, they could hear their own footsteps.

"I'll bet Dad's calling to say he's on his way," Ashley said.

When they reached the phone, Mary-Kate took the receiver first. "Hi, Dad!" she said.

"Hi, Dad!" Ashley called over Mary-Kate's shoulder.

"Hi, girls," he answered.

Mary-Kate wrinkled her nose. Their dad sounded fuzzy and far away.

"I think we have a bad connection," Mary-Kate said. Her eyes lit up. "Are you calling from your car?"

"I'm calling from South America." Her dad sighed.

"South America?" Mary-Kate gasped. "Don't tell me your airline went on strike, too!"

7

She could see Ashley's mouth drop open.

"No," her dad said. "Some students and I came down with this weird rain forest fever—"

"Dad!" Mary-Kate gasped. "You didn't pick up one of those poisonous frogs, did you?"

"No," he said. "But some of those rain forest mosquitoes can do a number on you."

Mary-Kate couldn't believe her dad was that ill. He hardly ever got sick.

"Don't worry, Dad," she said. "There'll be four of us to take good care of you. Ashley and I asked Cheryl and Elise to come back to Chicago with us!"

"Whoa!" her dad interrupted. "You know I'd love to have your friends over for Christmas, Mary-Kate. But I've got some bad news. I won't be able to come home for the holidays. I'm really sorry."

Mary-Kate froze. She could hear Ashley whispering, "What? What? What did he say?"

"The doctor here says we have to rest in the hospital for another week or two," he went on. "Then we'll be well enough to go home."

"Dad?" Mary-Kate asked slowly. "If you're not coming home for the holidays, does that mean Ashley and I aren't either?"

CHAPTER
TWO

"What do you mean we're not going home?" Ashley cried. She shook Mary-Kate's arm. "What's Dad saying?"

Mary-Kate held the receiver away. "Some mosquitoes bit Dad and his students," she said in a low voice. "Now they have to spend the holidays in some Amazon hospital!"

Ashley grabbed the receiver from her sister's hands. "Dad!" she blurted out. "I told you to use bug spray! Even between your toes!"

"I'll be okay," he said in a weary voice. "But I'm sorry you kids will have to spend Christmas at school."

School? The word hit Ashley like a ton of bricks.

"It's a joke, right, Dad?" Ashley asked. "You're outside in the parking lot—wearing that goofy Santa hat!"

"I wish I were," her dad said. "But I promise to visit as soon as I get back to the States."

Ashley felt pretty sick herself. She couldn't possibly imagine Christmas without her dad!

"It's okay, Dad." Ashley sighed. "As long as you get well. That's the important thing."

"Yeah, Dad!" Mary-Kate shouted into the receiver. "Just take your medicine and don't pick at your scabs. That's what you told us when we had the chicken pox!"

Ashley heard her dad laugh. It was a good sign. But after they said good-bye, she didn't feel like laughing at all.

"Christmas without Dad," Mary-Kate wailed as they walked back to their room. "And stuck in school!"

"Wait till we tell Cheryl and Elise." Ashley groaned. "They are going to be so bummed out."

Cheryl and Elise were waiting for the twins when they walked into Ashley's room.

"Was it okay with your dad?" Elise asked.

"We-ell." Ashley hesitated. "We've got good news and bad news."

"The good news is—Dad said he would love to have you guys over for the holidays," Mary-Kate explained.

"Yes!" Elise cheered.

"The bad news is," Ashley said, "nobody's going home for the holidays."

"What?" Cheryl cried.

"Not even us," Ashley went on. "Dad and his students have to stay in South America. They came down with some tropical illness."

All four girls sat on the floor. They rested their chins on their hands.

No one said anything.

Ashley felt terrible, too. But she felt even worse moping.

"Hey, you guys," Ashley said. "Maybe being stuck at school won't be so bad."

Mary-Kate, Cheryl, and Elise all looked at Ashley in disbelief.

"What? Are you kidding?" Mary-Kate asked.

"Think about it," Ashley said. "Some guys from Harrington are probably stuck at school, too. And girls from the other classes."

"True," Cheryl said, brightening up.

"We'll also have Porter House to ourselves," Elise added. "No sharing bathrooms. And snooty

11

Dana Woletsky and her friends will be miles away."

Ashley nodded. Her pep talk was doing the trick!

"Plus Mrs. Pritchard will be around," Ashley added. "She usually does a good job at keeping us busy."

Mary-Kate jumped up. "We almost forgot," she said. "Mrs. Pritchard wanted to talk to us in her office."

"Maybe about some neat dance she has planned," Ashley said excitedly.

The girls pulled on their jackets, scarves, and hats. Then they hurried through the snowy campus toward Main House and Mrs. Pritchard's office.

"Come in," Mrs. Pritchard called after Ashley knocked on her door.

Mrs. Pritchard sat behind her desk. Her brown hair was brushed in a perfect pageboy. Fastened to her navy blue suit was a green and red holly-berry pin.

As they neared her desk Ashley noticed something else. Travel brochures—of the Hawaiian Islands!

"Hawaii!" Ashley exclaimed. "I'll bet that's the theme of our holiday party. Right, Mrs. Pritchard?"

Before Mrs. Pritchard could answer, the twins started singing and dancing a hula. Cheryl and Elise joined in, swaying across the floor.

" 'Oh, we're going to a hukilau!' " Mary-Kate sang. " 'A huki huki, huki lau—' "

"Ahem!" Mrs. Pritchard cleared her throat.

Everyone stopped dancing.

"This isn't for a party," Mrs. Pritchard said with a smile. "You see, my husband and I are going to Hawaii for Christmas. To visit our niece, Anna."

"Does that mean you're leaving?" Ashley asked slowly.

"As in—aloha?" Mary-Kate gulped.

"I'm afraid so, girls," Mrs. Pritchard said.

"But who's going to stick around with us?" Mary-Kate cried.

"That's what I wanted to explain to you all," Mrs. Pritchard said. "There aren't enough students to keep White Oak open for the holidays. So I've arranged to have all the girls stay at various Harrington dorms."

"You mean we'll be up close and personal with the boys?" Ashley asked.

"Not that close," Mrs. Pritchard warned. "Boys and girls will be rooming on different floors."

"Good!" Cheryl said. "I have three brothers, and you don't want to be too close to their socks."

Mrs. Pritchard began standing up. "There will be an acting housemother at the Harrington dorm," she said. "A teacher who volunteered to stay for the holidays."

Ashley could hear someone singing in the hallway. "Oh, there's no place like school for the holidays!" the woman's voice chirped.

"Who's that?" Mary-Kate asked.

She got her answer when a petite woman with pink hair appeared at the door. She was wearing a short black dress with candy-cane-striped stockings. Hanging from her ears were earrings shaped like Christmas ball ornaments.

Ashley smiled. It was Ms. Keech, the art teacher. Ms. Keech was cool. She loved cracking jokes and always came up with the neatest projects.

"Well, what are you girls waiting for?" Ms. Keech asked, her hands on her hips. "Let's get packing for Harrington country. Yeeee-haaaa!"

"You're our housemother?" Mary-Kate asked.

"Yeah, but don't call me mom," Ms. Keech said. She pretended to whisper. "Or I'll make you clean your room and eat all your vegetables!"

The girls laughed as Ms. Keech wiggled her earrings and slipped out the door.

"You see?" Ashley said. "I told you this was going to be a great Christmas!"

They were about to high-five, when a girl

14

dressed in a suede coat with a fake-fur collar marched in. It was Kristen Lindquist, Dana Woletsky's best and snootiest friend!

Kristen flipped her blond hair over her shoulder. "Look who's stuck here for Christmas," she said.

"Don't you have a plane to catch, Kristen?" Mary-Kate asked, pretending to look at her watch.

"I wish!" Kristen grumbled. "It's a good thing I look good in orange. Because that's what all fashionable inmates are wearing this year."

Kristen marched over to the mirror hanging over Mrs. Pritchard's side table. As she smoothed her lip gloss with her pinkie, Ashley and the others began to whisper.

"Inmates?" Elise repeated. "What does that mean?"

"It means Kristen is stuck at school, too," Cheryl said. "And we're stuck with her!"

Mary-Kate looked at Ashley and frowned. "A great Christmas, huh?" she mumbled.

Ashley shrugged. "Hey, I said Christmas would be okay," she whispered. "I didn't say it would be perfect!"

CHAPTER THREE

"Here we are, ladies!" Ms. Keech said as she drove the van through the Harrington campus on Monday. "Your new home away from home!"

Mary-Kate rubbed the frosty car window to peek outside. She and Ashley had been on the Harrington campus many times for classes. But it never looked so empty!

"Where is everybody?" Elise asked.

"Probably partying," Ashley said cheerily. "Which is what we are going to do for the next two weeks!"

Mary-Kate smiled. The thought of nonstop partying didn't seem so bad. Even with Kristen!

"Let's have pizza parties!" Mary-Kate suggested.

"And rent a bunch of videos. And play Twister with the boys."

"The boys!" Elise repeated. "I've never been inside a boys' dorm before."

"I have," Kristen said coolly. "One time Dana and I dressed in boys' clothes and we snuck into the East dorm—"

Ms. Keech gave Kristen a hard stare in the rearview mirror.

"Kidding!" Kristen said quickly.

Mary-Kate rolled her eyes. Everyone knew that Kristen was boy crazy. She collected boyfriends like Elise collected glitter accessories!

Ms. Keech drove the van to the dorm block. Other girls were unloading their bags. Many of the boys rushed out to help them.

"I wonder what guys will greet us," Ashley said dreamily. "Phillip Jacoby? Peter Juarez?"

"Ross Lambert?" Mary-Kate joked.

Ashley blushed at the mention of her boyfriend.

"Keep your eyes peeled for Wesley House, girls," Ms. Keech called over her shoulder. "That's the first-form dorm we'll be staying in." The first-year students were called first-formers. Mary-Kate and Ashley and their friends were all first-formers.

Mary-Kate saw a big white mansion in the distance. "I hope that's it," she said, pointing.

"Not likely!" Ms. Keech laughed. "That's the Harrington mansion. All of the Harrington ancestors lived there. Including the school's founder, Phineas T. Harrington III."

"But the house looks totally empty," Elise said.

"That's because Mr. and Mrs. Harrington went to Rome for the holidays," Ms. Keech explained.

"Just as well." Kristen sniffed. "I heard all the Harringtons are total snobs."

"So did I," Elise said. "So who needs them?"

The van stopped in front of a cream-colored house with green shutters. A sign over the door read Wesley House.

As the girls pulled their bags out of the van, Mary-Kate noticed a white sheet hanging from a window of the next dorm. Painted on it was the word HELP!!!

"Hmm," Ashley said. "Maybe they ran out of garlic for their pizza."

The girls were about to carry their bags to the door, when a second-form boy came over. He whispered, "Escape now. Before it's too late!"

"What's going on here?" Mary-Kate asked Ashley as the boy took off. "Help? Escape?"

"Must be some kind of joke!" Ashley said, grinning. "You know, for us 'new kids.'"

All the bags were finally unloaded. The girls waited outside Wesley while Ms. Keech parked the van.

Kristen flung back her red cashmere scarf, almost hitting Mary-Kate in the mouth. "Wait till the boys see us," she said. "They are going to be so psyched!"

The front door opened and four boys marched out. They stood on the doorstep with their arms folded.

"Or . . . maybe not," Kristen said.

Mary-Kate checked out the boys. She didn't know any of them. Three wore T-shirts with computer game logos. The fourth wore an Albert Einstein sweatshirt.

"Hi," Mary-Kate said, smiling widely. "We're all here from White Oak. Porter House."

The boys nodded. Then they barked out their names one by one—"Garth Mitchell" "Derek Wang" "Victor Nichols" "Tyrone Hicks."

Mary-Kate blinked as the boys turned and began walking back into the house.

"Hey, what's the rush?" Ashley called. "We're going to be neighbors, you know."

"I hope you like Twister," Mary-Kate said.

"What's that?" Derek asked.

"It's a game!" Mary-Kate said.

"Does it run on double-A batteries?" Tyrone asked.

"How impressive is its resolution?" Derek asked.

"Does it include a thirty-two-bit RISC-CPU with embedded memory?" Garth asked.

"Does it have a color LCD screen?" Victor asked. "And a sound chip that supports stereo playback?"

Silence.

"Um . . . you put it on the floor. It has . . . colored dots," Mary-Kate replied.

"Oh," the boys said at the same time.

Mary-Kate's shoulders dropped. So much for pizza parties, videos, and most of all—Twister.

Ms. Keech hurried over carrying a cardboard box.

"Look lively, kids," she said. "'Tis the season to be jolly. So let's deck the halls!"

The girls looked inside the box. It was stuffed with holiday decorations.

"Glitter bells!" Elise gasped.

"Fake snow!" Cheryl exclaimed.

Even the boys walked over to check it out.

"Hmmm, tinsel," Derek said, pulling out a strand. "You know it reminds me of the substance the aliens used to entrap Captain Bowen on Planet Nemesis!"

"An excellent computer game!" Tyrone confirmed.

Mary-Kate watched the boys give each other high fives and walk into the house.

"Just our luck," Mary-Kate said. "The only first-form boys stuck at school are computer geeks."

Kristen tilted her head. "The one with the Albert Einstein sweatshirt is kind of cute," she said.

"Kristen!" Elise complained. "Is that all you can think about?"

An hour later everyone got together to decorate the main floor. And it really broke the ice.

Mary-Kate and Ashley worked together at hanging holly-berry wreaths on all the doors. The boys did a great job at flinging tinsel over the bulletin boards.

"Remember to save some decorations for the big holiday party at the end of the week," Ms. Keech reminded them. "It's a school tradition, you know."

"Speaking of tradition," Mary-Kate said, "let's go outside and decorate a tree. We can pick some kind of theme . . . like sports!"

"Nah!" Garth scoffed. "How about we do the solar system?"

"Unh-unh!" Mary-Kate said, smiling. "Sports!"

"No way! Solar system!" Garth argued.

Mary-Kate wasn't about to give in. She grabbed a few strands of tinsel and playfully flung it over Garth's head.

"Go, Mary-Kate!" Ashley cheered.

Garth grinned as he grabbed his own handful of tinsel. He was about to fling it on Mary-Kate when—

"Stop it at once!" a gruff voice demanded.

Everyone spun around.

A tall man stood behind them. He was wearing glasses with tortoiseshell frames and a white shirt. The waistband of his pants was tugged up to the middle of his chest and his shoes were polished to a blinding gleam.

"And take down those decorations!" he snapped. "It may be the holidays, but this is still a school."

Mary-Kate and Ashley stared at the man as he turned on his heel and marched down the hall.

"Who was that grump?" Ashley whispered.

"That's the acting headmaster," Garth whispered back. "His name is Charles Turnbull."

"No, it's not," Mary-Kate said. "His name is Scrooge! And there goes our Merry Christmas."

CHAPTER FOUR

"Bah, humbug!" Ashley groaned as they tore down the decorations. "No wonder those kids hung out the HELP!!! sign."

"Yeah," Mary-Kate said, ripping a paper snowflake off the wall. "This isn't Harrington—it's a maximum security prison."

"I'm sorry, kids," Ms. Keech said. "I didn't know that Mr. Turnbull was so . . . so . . . "

"Horrible," Cheryl filled in.

"Now, I'm sure Mr. Turnbull is a perfectly nice guy," Ms. Keech chirped. "He's probably just having a bad day."

"A bad day?" Derek muttered. "He's been having a bad day since he got here a year ago."

Everyone worked hard to clear away any trace of decoration. When they were done, Mr. Turnbull returned to inspect. "Better, better," he said, nodding his head.

"Would you like us to save the decorations for the holiday party, Mr. Turnbull?" Ms. Keech asked.

"What party?" Mr. Turnbull asked with a sour face.

"Uh-oh," Mary-Kate whispered to Ashley.

"That was the last acting-headmaster's tradition, not mine," Mr. Turnbull said. "Instead, we'll wash dishes at the local soup kitchen. It will be a satisfying experience."

"Is it too late for me to get a bus ticket?" Cheryl muttered.

"Are there buses that go to Fiji?" Elise whispered.

"Any questions?" Mr. Turnbull asked.

"Just one," Mary-Kate said. "Can we at least use the rec room? And the gym? And the library?"

"I'm afraid not," Mr. Turnbull said. "All of the buildings have been locked for the holidays. Except the dining room, of course."

"But what are we going to do?" Elise asked. "You know . . . for fun?"

"Good question," Mr. Turnbull said. He pointed

to a stack of books piled high in the hallway. "This will be a splendid time to catch up on our studies, don't you think?"

Ashley stared at Mary-Kate. *He's got to be kidding*, she thought.

"Oh, where's your holiday spirit, Mr. Turnbull?" Ms. Keech asked. She smiled and pumped her fist.

"I have plenty of spirit," Mr. Turnbull said. "In celebration of the holiday season, I've arranged to have eggnog oatmeal served every morning."

Please tell me this isn't happening, Ashley thought.

"I expect the girls to unpack immediately," Mr. Turnbull said. "And the boys to clean their rooms."

Everyone stood openmouthed as Mr. Turnbull turned and walked away. Ms. Keech ran after him.

"What are we going to do now?" Mary-Kate wailed. "We can't use the rec room. Or the gym. Or anything else."

Ashley gazed outside the glass door. The snow on the ground gave her an idea. "I know what we can do," she said. "Let's have a snowball fight!"

"Get real, Ashley," Mary-Kate said. "Turnbull would flip if he saw us doing that."

"He never said anything about goofing around in the snow," Ashley pointed out. "And we've got time to unpack."

25

"I don't know," Kristen said. She wiggled her fingers. "I might ruin my manicure."

Garth stared at his hand. "And I might freeze my keyboard fingers," he said.

"Come on, Garth," Ashley said. "Now's your chance to get back at Mary-Kate for that tinsel attack."

"Let's see what you're made of!" Mary-Kate teased.

The kids pulled on their jackets and ran outside. When they reached a snowy field behind Wesley House they divided into teams—boys against the girls.

"Elise and Kristen will make the snowballs," Mary-Kate said. "Ashley, Cheryl, and I will throw them."

Soon both teams were pitching snowballs at one another at breakneck speed.

"Attack!" Victor yelled as he hauled a snowball. Ashley ducked, but not fast enough. She giggled as it exploded on her shoulder.

"Ready, aim, fire!" Mary-Kate shouted as she pitched a snowball at Tyrone. It knocked the earmuffs off his head and everyone laughed.

"Hey!" Mary-Kate said. "They didn't make me pitcher of the first-form softball team for nothing."

Mary-Kate spoke too soon. A snowball whizzed across the field and landed square on her forehead.

"Made you look! Made you look!" Garth cackled.

"This is going to be good," Ashley said as Mary-Kate picked up another snowball.

"Payback time!" Mary-Kate said, throwing her arm back.

The boys ducked and Ashley gasped. Standing behind them was a frowning Mr. Turnbull.

"Mary-Kate—don't!" Ashley cried.

Too late. Mary-Kate's snowball was whizzing through the air, headed for Mr. Turnbull's face.

SPLAT!

Mr. Turnbull slowly wiped the snow from his glasses. "What do you all think you're doing?" he demanded.

"G-g-getting some exercise?" Derek gulped.

"You were having a snowball fight," Mr. Turnbull said. "And snowball fights are off-limits!"

What isn't? Ashley wondered.

"In fact," Mr. Turnbull went on, "there will be no building of snowmen either!"

"What's wrong with snowmen?" Elise asked.

"Snowmen melt," Mr. Turnbull snapped. "And I will not have the campus strewn with soggy carrots and top hats."

"Oh, well," Ashley said as Turnbull stomped back through the snow. "At least we got to have a few minutes of fun."

The girls nodded. But the boys were silent.

"Come on, guys," Garth said. "Let's go."

"What's with them?" Ashley asked as she watched the boys trudge back to the dorm without saying good-bye.

"Who knows?" Mary-Kate said. "They're probably as bummed out as we are."

The girls headed back to Wesley House to unpack. Ms. Keech showed them to their assigned rooms.

"We're roomies!" Mary-Kate said happily as they entered a sunny room with big windows.

Ashley looked around. The boys' room was abandoned for the holidays. It had twin beds separated by a tall wooden dresser. There were two desks and lots of posters on the walls.

"Hey, look!" Mary-Kate said, pointing to a poster of Sammy Sosa. "These guys like the Cubs."

Ashley pointed to another poster of a blond singer wearing flare pants and a short midriff blouse.

"That's not all they like." Ashley giggled.

The girls unpacked their bags. Mary-Kate folded

most of her clothes and laid them in the bureau. Ashley carefully hung her outfits in the closet. When they were done, they joined the others in the hallway.

"What do we do the rest of the week?" Cheryl asked.

"Let's find the guys," Mary-Kate said. "Maybe they have some neat ideas."

The girls found the boys in the Wesley lounge. Derek and Garth were holding electronic games. Tyrone and Victor were busily tapping away on their laptops.

Mary-Kate looked over Garth's shoulder. "Who's winning?" she asked. "Space Freaks or Morons from Mars?"

Garth didn't answer.

"Okay." Mary-Kate shrugged. She walked over to a boom box and flicked it on. The music of the twins' favorite group filled the room.

"4-You!" Ashley cheered. "Crank it up!"

The girls began dancing and singing along. Garth threw down his game and jumped up.

"Stop stomping!" Garth cried. "You just hurled my spacecraft eight million light-years from Planet Earth. Now I'll never get back."

"Yeah. I can't program my computer with all that

background noise going on," Derek complained.

"Come on, guys," Cheryl urged. "Why don't you kick back and have some fun?"

"We tried having fun your way," Garth said. "And it got us into trouble."

The boys went back to their computers and games.

"I can't believe it!" Kristen cried as they left the lounge. "No boy has ever wanted me to leave before. Ever!"

Ashley plopped down on the staircase.

Dad gets sick. Mr. Turnbull's a monster. And the boys here are geeks, she thought. *Can the holidays get any worse?*

CHAPTER FIVE

"It's hopeless." Ashley sighed from the staircase.

"It is not!" Mary-Kate said. "Just because the guys don't want to be with us doesn't mean we can't have fun."

"But they practically banned us from the lounge, Mary-Kate," Cheryl exclaimed.

"So what?" Mary-Kate shrugged. She leaned on the banister and grinned. "Let's find our own place to hang out."

"Where?" Ashley asked.

"Well, we're not going to find it sitting here!" Mary-Kate declared. She grabbed Ashley's hand and pulled her up.

Mary-Kate led everyone up the staircase—until

she saw Mr. Turnbull posting a list of rules on the second floor.

"Retreat!" Mary-Kate ordered.

The girls stampeded back to the main floor.

"Where now?" Ashley asked.

Mary-Kate's eyes darted up and down the hall. Next to the pay phone was a door they hadn't opened yet.

"It's probably a broom closet," Cheryl said as Mary-Kate tugged at the door.

The door was sticky but after a few yanks it flew wide open. Mary-Kate peered through. It was dark but she could make out a staircase leading down to another door.

"Let's see what's down there," Mary-Kate suggested.

Kristen's platform boots made loud clunking sounds as the girls went down the stairs.

Mary-Kate grunted as she pushed open the next door. It was dark inside but she found a light switch.

Mary-Kate flicked on the light—and gasped.

The room was filled with tons of old stuff—rusty bicycles, dusty piles of yearbooks, neon-colored eight-track tape players from the seventies—even an old Charlie's Angels pinball machine and a jukebox!

"Cool!" Ashley cried as she walked deeper into the room. "This has got to be the storage room!"

"You mean the museum!" Cheryl joked as she held up a lava lamp.

Mary-Kate gave a thumbs-up sign. "This is it," she said. "The perfect place to hang out."

"Look at all the cute guys with the long side-burns!" Kristen said, flipping through a yearbook.

"Kristen!" Cheryl said. "Those guys are our fathers' age now!"

"Ewww!" Kristen said, dropping the book.

Mary-Kate and Ashley headed for the jukebox shaped like a big neon shell. Mary-Kate pulled a quarter from her jeans pocket. Then she announced in a pretend-deejay-voice:

"The White Oak disco is ready to get down! So all you dancing queens with boogie fever—it's time to shake your groove thing to . . . "

Mary-Kate pressed B14. " . . . 'Disco Duck'!"

The girls watched for the handle to scoop up the vinyl record. But nothing happened.

"It's probably not plugged in," Mary-Kate said. "Help me move this clunker and find an outlet."

All five girls grunted as they pushed the dusty jukebox to the side. They didn't find a plug. But they did find another door.

"There's got to be more neat stuff behind there!" Mary-Kate said.

The door seemed stuck. But after a few thrusts, Mary-Kate pushed it open. She looked inside. Another staircase!

"I'm not going down there." Ashley shuddered. "There are probably rats—or bats—or worse!"

"You're just being chicken!" Mary-Kate joked.

"I am not!" Ashley insisted. "It's just that it's pitch-black down there."

"Not anymore," Kristen said. She reached into the pocket of her suede vest and pulled out a pen. Pressing a button on the side, she made it light up.

"A flashlight pen?" Mary-Kate asked.

"So I can write in my diary after lights-out," Kristen explained.

"Gee, thanks, Kristen," Ashley grumbled as she followed the others down the stairs.

Kristen shone her penlight this way and that. "Wow. This is some kind of tunnel," she said.

"Let's see where it leads," Mary-Kate said excitedly.

The girls walked slowly through the tunnel. The farther they walked, the lighter the tunnel became.

"Check out the graffiti," Mary-Kate said. She strained her eyes to read the scrawl on the wall.

"'Please Join the War on Poverty,'" Elise read out

loud. "'Increase My Allowance!'" She giggled.

"There must have been students down here," Ashley said. "A long time ago."

They walked to the end of the tunnel and turned a corner. It led to another tunnel. But this one was different. There was a lit lightbulb hanging from the ceiling, sports posters on the walls, pillows on the floor, and stacks of books and electronic games.

"Signs of intelligent life," Mary-Kate said.

"This is too weird!" Ashley said. "Let's head back."

"Come on, Ashley!" Mary-Kate said. "I thought you liked a little adventure."

"Sure," Ashley said. "In a movie theater with a bag of popcorn on my lap. I'm out of here." Ashley pointed to a door between two Red Sox posters. "Maybe that door leads to a shortcut upstairs."

"Or another tunnel!" Mary-Kate said excitedly. She grabbed the doorknob.

Giving it a yank, the door flew open.

Mary-Kate blinked. Looming in the doorway was a tall, dark shadow!

She opened her mouth to scream.

But Ashley beat her to it. . . .

"Aahhhhh!"

CHAPTER SIX

Mary-Kate grabbed Kristen's penlight and beamed it on the shadowy figure.

"Hey!" A boy of about fourteen stepped into view. As he brought his hand over his eyes he dropped a jar of jalapeño bean dip on the hard floor.

"Oh, great," the boy groaned. Green dip oozed over his shiny shoe. "That was the last jar of extra-spicy."

Mary-Kate studied the boy. Under his other arm was a bag of tortilla chips. He was dressed in a dark green V-neck sweater and beige pants. His hair was neatly slicked back with gel and the frames on his glasses were tortoiseshell.

"Who are you?" Mary-Kate asked the boy. "Are

you from another dorm? What's your name?"

"First the light—now the interrogation," the boy said, shaking his head.

Mary-Kate watched as the boy scraped dip off his shoe and stepped forward.

"My name's Colton," he said.

"Do you go to Harrington?" Elise asked.

"Used to," Colton replied. His face dropped. "Until my mom and dad were charged by rhinos on an African picture-taking safari."

Mary-Kate and the others froze.

Elise gasped. "How awful!"

"How did you end up down here of all places?" Mary-Kate asked.

Colton ran his hand through his hair.

"After the accident I had a choice," Colton explained. "Everyone said I had to live with my aunt Gladys in Milwaukee. But I decided to hide down here in the Harrington tunnels."

"What was wrong with Aunt Gladys?" Mary-Kate asked.

"Not much," Colton said. "Except for the polka-dancing school she had in the basement. And her seventy-five cats."

"Wow!" Cheryl whistled.

"But wasn't your aunt worried when you never

showed up at her house?" Ashley asked.

"No." Colton sighed. "Aunt Gladys had an accident, too."

"What happened?" Elise asked.

"She dropped an accordion on her foot. When she found out she could never polka again . . . she went a little crazy. She sort of forgot all about me."

Complete silence.

Colton plopped down on a pillow and stretched his long legs. "These tunnels were built way back in the 1800s. That way students could go from one building to another on cold and snowy days," he explained.

"How come we never knew about them?" Mary-Kate asked.

"They were shut down about thirty years ago," Colton went on. "They've been kept a secret from all the new kids ever since. The heads didn't want the guys to find them and use them for parties."

"Then how did you know?" Ashley asked.

"Me?" Colton said. He smiled. "Can we cut the questions, please?"

"One more," Mary-Kate said. "If nobody knows you live down here, how do you survive?"

"Glad you asked," Colton said. He stood up and pointed his hand in the direction of the door. "Follow me."

"Mary-Kate!" Ashley pulled her sister aside. "Are you sure this is a good idea? We don't know where he's taking us."

"I think he's okay," Mary-Kate whispered. "He seems kind of nice."

Colton led the girls up another staircase. He opened a door and waved everyone through.

"Ta-daaa!" Colton sang.

Mary-Kate looked around. There was a Ping-Pong table, video games, snack machines, and a big-screen TV!

"Hey, I know where we are," Mary-Kate exclaimed. "It's the Harrington rec room!"

"And there are other underground tunnels leading to the kitchen, the library, and the pool," Colton said.

"The pool!" Mary-Kate said. She nudged Ashley. "Good thing you packed your bathing suit, huh?"

Ashley gave Mary-Kate a weak smile.

But the other girls jumped up and down.

"Happy holidays!" Cheryl cheered.

"Are you stuck here at school for the holidays?" Colton asked them.

"Yeah," Elise said. "But now that we found these tunnels, it won't be so bad."

"Right," Kristen agreed. "Wait until the guys

find out about this. They'll want to hang with us for sure."

"Not so fast!" Colton said. "These tunnels are my underground lair. My secret. You're not going to tell more kids, are you?"

Mary-Kate didn't know what to say. She felt sorry for Colton. And besides . . . he was kind of cute.

"You guys," Mary-Kate whispered. "Colton trusted us with his secret. If he doesn't want us to blab, then let's not blab."

Ashley, Cheryl, and Elise nodded. Kristen folded her arms and rolled her eyes.

"Your secret is safe with us, Colton," Mary-Kate said. "But since we already know about the tunnels, we might as well use them."

"You mean . . . every day?" Colton asked.

"It'll just be for two weeks," Mary-Kate explained. "And who knows? You might even get used to our company."

"Company," Colton whistled. "I haven't had company for almost a year."

"So what do you say?" Mary-Kate asked.

"Okay," Colton said. "It's a deal."

Colton reached to shake Mary-Kate's hand. As she grabbed it, she looked into his dark brown eyes.

They seemed to sparkle behind his glasses. His smile slanted a bit. Like those models in the Gap ads.

"We'd better get back!" Ashley interrupted Mary-Kate's thoughts. "Or Terrible Turnbull will be on our case."

Turnbull who? Mary-Kate thought dreamily.

"Wait!" Colton said. He pulled a bunch of quarters from his pocket and ran to the snack machine.

"Take these with you!" Colton said as five candy bars tumbled out. "Happy holidays!"

"Caramel crunch!" Cheryl cried. "Way to go!"

Hmm, Mary-Kate thought as he handed out the candy bars. *I wonder where he got all those quarters.* She brushed away the thought.

"We'll be here tomorrow, Colton," Mary-Kate said when they were back down in the tunnel.

"Same time, same place," Colton added.

The girls retraced their steps back to Wesley.

"I still don't like this," Ashley said. "There's something about Colton that I don't trust."

"And why can't we tell the boys?" Kristen asked. "What fun is a rec room without boys? What fun is anything without boys?"

"Because we made a promise to Colton," Mary-Kate pointed out. "And a promise is a promise."

"I agree with Ashley," Kristen said. "Colton is a weirdo. Who else lives underground all year long?"

"He must come up once in a while," Elise said. "For special occasions."

"Yeah," Kristen joked. "Groundhog Day!"

Mary-Kate glared at Kristen. "Colton is a nice kid with a big secret, Kristen," she said. "And now he's our secret, too."

But as they climbed the stairs back to the storage room, Mary-Kate knew she had a secret of her own. She was getting a major crush on Colton!

CHAPTER SEVEN

"He reminds me of someone," Ashley said at dinner that night. She picked at her macaroni and cheese with her fork.

"Who?" Elise asked.

"Colton. But I can't figure out who," Ashley said. She turned to her sister. "Can you, Mary-Kate?"

"Hmmm?" Mary-Kate asked absentmindedly.

"Never mind." Ashley sighed.

"Time for dessert!" Cheryl announced. She pulled a caramel crunch bar from her sweater pocket. "Compliments of our underground hero."

Ashley pulled her own candy bar from her jeans pocket. She tore open the wrapper and took a big bite. But the gooey caramel and creamy chocolate couldn't keep her from worrying about the tunnels.

"How do we keep the guys from noticing we're gone when we go back to those tunnels?" Ashley asked.

"The guys?" Mary-Kate snorted. "They couldn't care less about us."

"That's what you think," Kristen said. She sat up straight and smoothed her hair. "Here they come."

The boys sauntered over.

"Where did you get these candy bars?" Garth asked. "The snack machine in the lounge has been out of chocolate bars since last week."

"Haven't you heard of Care packages?" Kristen piped up. She held out her candy bar. "You can have the rest of mine. Chocolate gives me zits."

Garth wrinkled his nose and shook his head. "Sharing food spreads germs. No thanks."

Kristen stared at her candy bar as the boys walked back to their own table.

"The boys aren't our biggest problem," Cheryl said. "Mr. Turnbull might still catch on."

Ashley saw Mr. Turnbull sitting in the front of the dining room. He was frowning and cutting his macaroni into tiny little pieces.

"Unless," Ashley said slowly, "we find a way to keep Mr. Turnbull busy."

"Too bad he doesn't have a girlfriend," Kristen said.

"What woman would be crazy enough to hook up with Turnbull?" Cheryl said.

"Oh, the weather outside is frightful," a singing voice interrupted. "But this pie is so delightful!"

Ashley turned and saw Ms. Keech. She was walking through the dining room carrying a tray filled with pies and pudding.

"Hi, girls," Ms. Keech called, her candy-cane earrings dangling. "Start with dessert, I always say."

As Ms. Keech headed for a table in the back, Ashley turned to the others. "Ms. Keech!" she declared. "The perfect match!"

"Ms. Keech and Mr. Turnbull?" Mary-Kate cried. "They're like a toy poodle and—a pit bull!"

"Different people hook up all the time," Ashley said. "It happens in the movies."

"Yeah," Cheryl scoffed. "Beauty and the beast!"

"It's the only way to get Turnbull out of our hair," Ashley insisted. "Well? What do you think?"

Mary-Kate thought about it. Then she grinned.

"It's crazy," she said. "But it just might work!"

"Mary-Kate." Ashley sat up in bed. "Aren't you going to sleep? Lights-out was half an hour ago."

"Not yet," Mary-Kate said. She was writing Christmas cards to her friends in Chicago. "I have one more to write."

"Who are you writing to?" Ashley asked, curious. She picked up a card from the night table and opened it.

"Dear Amanda," Ashley read out loud. "Christmas at school won't be a total bust after all. If you could only see the cute guy—"

"Hey!" Mary-Kate cried. She snatched the card out of Ashley's hand.

"What hot guy?" Ashley asked. "Garth? Tyrone?"

"Get a life!" Mary-Kate protested. She took her pillow and flung it at Ashley.

Then Ashley got it.

"Colton!" Ashley gasped.

Mary-Kate shrugged. "He *is* kind of cute."

"And kind of strange," Ashley added. "I mean— what kid lives underground for almost a year? And where does he get his clothes?"

"Catalogues?" Mary-Kate guessed.

Ashley groaned and tossed the pillow back at Mary-Kate. She flopped back on her own pillow.

Oh, great! Ashley thought with a frown. *Mary-Kate's in love. With a guy who lives in a tunnel!*

CHAPTER EIGHT

"Remember," Ashley told Elise Tuesday morning. "We have to convince Ms. Keech that Mr. Turnbull is really cute." She frowned. "Or at least interesting."

"I know you're a good reporter, Ashley," Elise said. "But are you good at fiction?"

Ashley rolled her eyes. "Come on," she said, starting down the stairs. But when they got to the landing, Ashley froze.

Mr. Turnbull was on the main floor—taping up the candy machine!

"No junk food on my watch," he was muttering. "If they want to snack, let them eat celery!"

Ashley shuddered. "He's evil, all right," she

47

whispered. "What will make Ms. Keech fall for him?"

The girls tiptoed past Mr. Turnbull. As they made their way down the hall, Ashley could hear Ms. Keech singing sweetly.

"Dashing through the snow," she sang. "In a freaky storm in May—"

"It's Ms. Keech!" Ashley whispered. "It sounds like she's in the sitting room."

Ashley and Elise peeked into the sitting room. Ms. Keech was sitting at her easel dressed in red overalls and a bright green turtleneck. Wrapped around her hair was a headband with a bright holly-berry print.

"Hi, Ms. Keech," Ashley said as she and Elise entered the room. "Can we see what you're painting today?"

"You bet," Ms. Keech said. She dropped a brush in a coffee can filled with water. "I was just finishing my latest abstract."

Ashley tilted her head and studied the painting. All she saw was a bunch of white dashes over a brown background. "What . . . is it?" she asked.

"It's a herd of polar bears in a mud slide," Ms. Keech explained. "Can't you see it?"

Elise peered at the canvas. "I can!" she said excitedly. "Look at their cute little paws and tiny noses."

Ashley blinked. *Where?*

"And guess what?" Ms. Keech said. "I'm going to ask Mr. Turnbull if we can all paint. Wouldn't that be great?"

Ashley jumped at the sound of Mr. Turnbull's name. She thought fast.

"Um," Ashley said. "Speaking of Mr. Turnbull— I mean painting—did you ever try your hand at painting portraits?"

"Sure did!" Ms. Keech said. She held her thumb in front of Ashley's face. "Would you like me to paint you?"

"No!" Ashley said quickly. "I mean, no, thank you. You really ought to paint someone more challenging."

"More challenging?" Ms. Keech repeated.

"Sure," Ashley said. She paced the room and waved her arms. "A face with lots of crags. And crevices."

"Like Mount Rushmore!" Elise piped up.

"Like . . ." Ashley tapped her chin and pretended to think. Then she snapped her fingers. "Mr. Turnbull!"

"Turnbull?" Ms. Keech wrinkled her nose.

"Great idea, Ashley," Elise said. "Mr. Turnbull

could probably use a portrait. For his office."

"Mr. Turnbull," Ms. Keech said thoughtfully. "Come to think of it—he is a bit like Mount Rushmore!"

Ashley and Elise nodded.

"What a super idea!" Ms. Keech cried. She waved her brush in the air, almost splattering Ashley. "I'll ask Mr. Rushmore—I mean Mr. Turnbull—if he'll sit for me."

Ms. Keech ran out of the room. Ashley and Elise gave each other a high five.

"Congratulations, Ashley!" Elise said. "Ms. Keech fell for it!"

"Yeah." Ashley sighed. "Now let's hope Mr. Turnbull does, too."

Ashley kept her fingers crossed all morning.

"I haven't seen Mr. Turnbull around," Cheryl said when they all gathered on the main floor.

"He could be in another dorm," Elise suggested.

"Or he could be with Ms. Keech," Mary-Kate said. She turned to Ashley. "Did your plan work, Ashley?"

"I don't know yet," Ashley said.

Kristen called them from the end of the hallway. The girls ran to join her.

"Check it out!" Kristen whispered. She pointed to the sitting room.

Ashley and the others peeked inside.

Ms. Keech was at her easel again. But this time she wasn't painting polar bears. She was painting a man dressed in a toga and holding a sprig of grapes. She was painting Mr. Turnbull!

"It worked!" Ashley whispered. "That ought to keep him busy for a while."

"It sure will!" Mary-Kate said. She turned to the others and gave a thumbs-up. "Okay, all systems go.

"To the tunnels!"

CHAPTER NINE

"Are you sure all the boys are in the lounge?" Mary-Kate asked as they opened the door to the storage room.

"Positive," Elise said. "When I checked they were downloading elephant jokes on their computers."

The girls walked through the storage room and descended the next staircase to the tunnel. Mary-Kate's heart pounded at the thought of seeing Colton.

But what if Colton doesn't show up? Mary-Kate wondered. *What if he was just playing a joke on us? What if I never see him again?*

"Yo!" a boy's voice called.

Mary-Kate shined Kristen's penlight down the tunnel. Gliding toward them on a skateboard was Colton!

"Greetings!" Colton said, jumping off his skate-board. He was wearing cuffed jeans, a black sweater, and gray sneakers with black stripes.

"Hi, Colton," Mary-Kate said, flashing a smile.

"I thought we'd hit the kitchen today and pig out," Colton said. "Is that cool with you?"

"Bring it on," Mary-Kate said.

Colton leaned his skateboard against the wall and waved his hand. "This way."

The girls followed Colton.

"Did you notice Colton's clean, crisp clothes?" Ashley whispered to Mary-Kate. "Not too shabby for a guy who lives in a tunnel."

"So Colton's a neat freak," Mary-Kate said. "If he can get to the kitchen, the library, and the gym—he can get to the laundry room."

After turning a few corners and climbing another staircase, the kids were in the Harrington kitchen.

"Let's make peanut butter and jelly sandwiches," Elise suggested. "With marshmallow topping."

"Bor-ing!" Colton said. He opened a huge icebox and pulled out two bags of English muffins. "The Colton special today is—Pizza Muffins Mexicali!"

The girls followed Colton's cooking directions. They spooned mild salsa over the muffins. Then they laid down strips of Monterey Jack cheese.

When that was done, they scooped on the guacamole and a sprinkle of jalapeño peppers.

"Where did you learn how to make these?" Ashley asked.

Colton wiped his hands on a linen dish towel. "Before my folks went to Africa, they were gourmet chefs in Paris."

"And they made pizza muffins?" Ashley asked in disbelief.

"Hey, it beats frogs' legs," Mary-Kate told Ashley. "Right, Colton?"

"Right!" Colton laughed.

Ashley heaved a big sigh. She flung a spoonful of sour cream on her muffin and headed for the oven.

Colton walked over to Mary-Kate. Her stomach did a triple flip.

"Hey," Mary-Kate said with a smile.

"Thanks for coming to my defense," Colton said.

"Oh, Ashley's cool," Mary-Kate said. "She just likes to ask a lot of questions. That's why she's a reporter for the school paper."

"Do you like to write, too?" Colton asked.

"Mostly the sports section," Mary-Kate replied. "Especially when it's about softball and basketball."

Colton's eyes flew wide open.

"Basketball definitely rules," he said. "I'm great

at defense. But I can also sink a mean bucket."

"And I'm an awesome dribbler," Mary-Kate said. "Did you know the first basketball hoops were fruit baskets?"

"No way!" Colton laughed. "What was the first basketball—a cantaloupe?"

Mary-Kate laughed with Colton. But then she tilted her head and studied him. "Don't you miss it?" she asked.

"Miss what?" Colton asked.

"You know, everything!" Mary-Kate said. "Fresh air, friends, movies—even basketball."

"I have friends," Colton said with a smile. "And don't forget. I know how to get into the gym."

"Oh, yeah," Mary-Kate chuckled.

Colton's eyes lit up. "Why don't I take you to the gym one day? We'll shoot some hoops. Just me and you."

Me and you. The magic words!

"You're on," Mary-Kate said.

"Great," Colton said. He smiled, then walked over to help Cheryl with a soggy pizza muffin.

It's official, Mary-Kate thought excitedly. I like Colton and now he likes me!

Mary-Kate ran to tell Ashley.

"Guess what?" Mary-Kate said. "Colton is crazy

for basketball, too. And he wants to shoot hoops with me!"

Taking her muffins out of the oven, Ashley glanced at Colton. "I still think Colton reminds me of someone," she said. "But who?"

"Freddie Prinze Jr.?" Mary-Kate asked with a grin.

"Very funny," Ashley smirked.

"I don't get it, Ashley," Mary-Kate said. "Colton is cute, funny, and an awesome cook. And I don't have a boyfriend yet—so what is the problem?"

"For one thing," Ashley said, "his stories about himself and his family are totally extreme!"

"I know," Mary-Kate admitted. "They are kind of wild."

"Well, if you ask me," Ashley said. "I think there's more to Colton than meets the eye."

Maybe there is more to Colton than meets the eye, Mary-Kate thought. *And I can't wait to find out what it is!*

CHAPTER TEN

"Oh, no!" Kristen cried the next day in the science lab. Her shoulders shook as she peered into the microscope. "It's worse than I thought!"

"What is it, Kristen?" Ashley looked up from her own microscope. "A parasite? A fungus?"

"Split ends." Kristen sighed. She pulled a strand of her long hair from under the microscope.

Ashley rolled her eyes and returned to her own microscope. It was Wednesday and the third day of tunnel exploration. This time Colton had led them all the way to the science lab.

I don't care how much fun we're having, Ashley thought. *There's still something weird about Colton.*

And Mary-Kate refuses to see it!

"Thanks for bringing us here, Colton," Mary-Kate said.

"Yeah!" Cheryl said. She looked up from her microscope. "I never knew a dead horsefly could look so cool!"

Elise pushed her microscope away and rubbed her eye. "And I didn't know glitter could be so dazzling!"

Ashley's eyes darted from her microscope to Mary-Kate. She was walking over to Colton. Her hair brushed against Colton's shoulder as she looked at his microscope.

"And what are you looking at?" Mary-Kate asked.

Colton looked up into Mary-Kate's eyes. "Toe jam."

"Eww—gross!" Mary-Kate cried.

"Kidding!" Colton laughed.

"Hey, Colton!" Ashley interrupted. "Did you get good grades in science?"

"Huh?" Colton asked. He turned away from Mary-Kate. "Um . . . yeah. Mostly A's and A pluses."

"Are you serious?" Mary-Kate gasped.

"Sure," Colton said. "I must take after my great-grandmother. The Newman Prize winner."

"The what?" Ashley asked.

"My great-grandmother won the Newman Prize for science," Colton replied. "For some invention you might have heard of."

"What was it?" Mary-Kate asked.

Colton shrugged. "The pencil eraser."

"The pencil eraser," Mary-Kate exclaimed. "I use that!"

"Who doesn't?" Ashley asked. "And why haven't I heard of the Newman Prize before?"

Colton didn't answer. Instead, he pulled the slide from his microscope and stood up.

"I know," Colton said. "Let's head to the rec room for some Ping-Pong."

"Sure, but I'm warning you," Mary-Kate teased. "I play a mean game of Ping-Pong."

"So did my uncle," Colton said.

"Your uncle?" Ashley asked.

Colton nodded. "He won the international Ping-Pong championship in China thirty years ago."

"Cool," Mary-Kate said.

"And," Colton went on, "my mom and dad were track-and-field stars in college."

"Really?" Ashley asked. "Too bad they couldn't outrun those rhinos—"

"Ashley!" Mary-Kate cried, horrified.

"Sorry," Ashley muttered. "But I really think we

should go upstairs. It's almost time for lunch, and Ms. Keech can't work on that painting forever."

"Don't worry," Cheryl said. "First she'll do his portrait—then his statue!"

"Oh, good." Elise giggled. "The pigeons will have a field day with him!"

Everyone laughed—except Colton.

"Aw, come on," Colton said. "Mr. Turnbull is an okay guy. Just a little rough around the edges, that's all."

"How do you know Mr. Turnbull, Colton?" Ashley asked. "He came to Harrington after you moved into the tunnel."

Colton stared at Ashley.

"I may live down in the tunnels," Colton finally said. "But I know what's going on."

"I'm going back upstairs," Ashley said. She carried her microscope to the shelf to put it away. "Whether you guys want to or not."

"You can't go without us, Ashley," Elise said.

"It's okay," Colton said. "Ashley's right. It is close to lunch. We'll meet again tomorrow."

Everyone cleaned their slides and put their microscopes on the shelf. Then Colton led the girls out of the lab and into the tunnel.

When the girls were back in the storage room,

they pushed the jukebox in front of the door. Then Cheryl, Elise, and Kristen headed up the stairs to the main floor.

"Wait!" Ashley said, tugging Mary-Kate's arm.

"What now?" Mary-Kate asked.

"I saw the way you flirted with Colton," Ashley said. "You were so obvious!"

"Pretty good, huh?" Mary-Kate chuckled. "And you thought you were the expert."

But Ashley wasn't laughing.

"I'm serious, Mary-Kate," Ashley said. "There's something about Colton that doesn't add up."

"You're just being a major worrywart," Mary-Kate interrupted. She gave a little wave. "See you upstairs, Ashley."

Tired of arguing, Ashley flopped down on a white beanbag chair with red and blue peace signs.

Love has really turned Mary-Kate's head inside-out, Ashley thought glumly. *And I'm not being a worry-wart.*

I'm just being—a good sister!

CHAPTER ELEVEN

"Why not?" Kristen asked later at lunch. "Why can't we invite the boys to our table?"

"Because I hate elephant jokes," Elise said, taking two key lime pies off her tray.

Mary-Kate looked at the boys sitting at the next table. Then she had a scary thought.

"Kristen?" Mary-Kate asked slowly. "You're not planning to tell the boys about the tunnels, are you?"

Kristen stopped drizzling dressing on her salad. "Mary-Kate, I'm insulted!" She gasped. "I may like boys, but I am not a blab!"

"Okay," Mary-Kate said, looking around the table. "But, remember, no mention of the tunnels from anyone."

While Kristen went to get the boys, Mary-Kate's thoughts turned to Colton.

Suddenly Mary-Kate had a brainstorm. She would write Colton a Christmas card and tell him exactly how she felt about him.

Mr. Turnbull walked by just as Kristen came back with the boys. He stopped and pointed to Elise's tray.

"Why did you take two pies, young lady?" he demanded.

"Um . . . I really like pie," Elise said with a nervous laugh.

Turnbull opened his mouth to speak, when a pea flew over his head.

"There will be no food fights in the dining room!" Mr. Turnbull bellowed. "Just for that pea projectile, there will be no more special activities!"

What special activities? Mary-Kate wondered.

Mr. Turnbull narrowed his eyes at the students. "So you can all forget about washing dishes at the soup kitchen on Christmas!" He growled. "Now carry on." Then he marched over to his table.

"Did you hear that?" Mary-Kate asked. "Turnbull acted like we wanted to wash dishes on Christmas."

"That's not all that's weird," Cheryl said. "He's

crumbling crackers in his coffee instead of in his soup!"

"What's with him?" Elise asked.

"Haven't you noticed?" Garth asked. He put his tray on the table and sat down. "Turnbull's been losing it lately."

"Yeah," Derek said. "Where've you been?"

"Not paying attention?" Mary-Kate took a long sip of milk.

"No, I mean it," Derek said. "Where've you girls been all morning?"

Mary-Kate sputtered her milk. "Er," she said. She knew she had to change the subject—fast. "We were . . . trying to think of new elephant jokes in my room!"

"Did you say elephant jokes?" Derek asked.

"Yeah," Mary-Kate said. "Have you heard any good ones lately?"

"As a matter of fact, yes," Garth said. "Why aren't elephants allowed at the beach?"

"Why?" Mary-Kate asked.

"Because they can't keep their trunks up!" the boys answered in unison.

The other girls groaned.

"More!" Mary-Kate cried. She clasped her hands. "We just can't get enough."

"Please speak for yourself," Cheryl muttered.

"Okay," Garth said. He opened his laptop computer. "But I'll have to boot them up first. We have over two hundred, you know."

"T-t-two hundred?" Elise stammered.

"Great!" Mary-Kate said. "You guys do that and we'll meet up with you later."

Mary-Kate signaled the others to pick up their trays and put on their jackets.

"Are you nuts?" Ashley whispered to Mary-Kate. "Now we'll have to spend the whole afternoon sitting through two hundred elephant jokes!"

"Who cares?" Mary-Kate asked. "At least it'll keep the guys from asking too many questions."

The girls hurried past Mr. Turnbull's table. An open packet of ketchup accidentally dropped off Ashley's tray.

"You heard what I said about food fights," Mr. Turnbull snarled.

"It wasn't a food fight, Mr. Turnbull," Ashley said. "The ketchup fell off my tray."

"That's how they all start," Mr. Turnbull said. "And if it happens again, you and your housemates will be spending the rest of winter break in your rooms!"

CHAPTER TWELVE

"I can't believe it," Ashley said Thursday morning. "I can't believe we're back down in these stupid tunnels."

"You'll feel different," Mary-Kate assured her, "once Colton leads us to the swimming pool."

Mary-Kate ran to catch up with the others.

"Colton, Colton, Colton." Ashley sighed. "You would think he was some kind of—superhero!"

Ashley felt someone tap her shoulder. Spinning around, she shrieked. Colton was standing right behind her.

"Was it something I said?" he asked.

"Colton!" Mary-Kate exclaimed. She raced over and stepped in front of Ashley.

"I thought we'd hit the library today," Colton told the girls. "There's an awesome book there about the history of roller coasters."

"How do you know?" Ashley asked.

"My cousin wrote it," Colton said. "He broke the record for riding every roller coaster in the world."

Oh, brother, Ashley thought. *Does this guy ever run out of wild stories?*

But Mary-Kate seemed impressed.

"I love roller coasters," Mary-Kate gushed. "Especially the ones that go upside down."

"What are we waiting for?" Colton asked. He shone a flashlight down the tunnel. "Let's check it out."

Roller coasters, Ashley thought. *If you ask me, it's Colton who's taking us for a ride.*

Colton led the way through three long tunnels. They were about to turn a corner, when Cheryl pointed to a door.

"We haven't been through this one yet," Cheryl said.

Colton froze. He shook his head. "You don't want to go in there," he said.

"Why not?" Cheryl asked.

"I get it," Mary-Kate said, smiling. "You're saving this door for last—because it leads to the pool."

Mary-Kate pulled at the doorknob. The door had opened just an inch, when Colton grabbed her hand.

"It doesn't," Colton said firmly. He looked Mary-Kate straight in the eye. "Trust me."

Mary-Kate stared back at Colton. Pulling back her hand, she shut the door. "Okay," she said. "No problem."

Ashley and the others stared at Colton. What was behind that door? And why didn't he want them to see it?

"Onward, march," Colton said, suddenly acting cheerful.

The kids trekked through more tunnels until they finally reached the library.

"I'm going to hit the stacks and look for that roller-coaster book," Colton said.

The girls sat down at a table. But as soon as Colton disappeared, they began to whisper.

"Did you see that?" Cheryl asked. "What was Colton's problem with that door?"

"And what's behind that door, anyway?" Kristen asked.

"Maybe Colton's stashing away secret Harrington files," Elise said, wide-eyed. "Maybe he's a spy!"

"I told you there was something strange about him," Ashley said. "I told you!"

"Time out!" Mary-Kate said. "There's probably nothing weird behind that door."

"How do you know?" Ashley asked.

"I don't," Mary-Kate said. "But let's find out."

Ashley raised an eyebrow. "You mean . . . ?"

"Let's sneak down to the tunnels tonight." Mary-Kate nodded. "I'll open the door and we'll find out what's behind there."

"What if Colton sees us?" Ashley asked.

"That door is nowhere near where Colton hangs out," Mary-Kate said. "Well? Do you want to do it? Or not?"

Ashley looked around the table. The others were nodding in agreement.

"We'll meet on the main floor after lights-out," Mary-Kate whispered. "Ms. Keech is usually in bed by then."

"Hey! What's with the whispering?"

Ashley jumped when she heard Colton's voice.

"I said, what's with the whispering?" Colton asked as he walked over with a book under his arm.

"Um . . . it's a library!" Ashley said. "Habit, I guess."

Colton placed the book on the table. He took off

his sweater and draped it over the back of a chair.

"Check it out," Colton said, opening the book to the first page. "You probably never rode coasters like these."

Everyone but Ashley gazed at the book.

"Wow—that one goes upside down all the way." Mary-Kate gasped. "Take a look, Ashley."

"No thanks," Ashley said. "Coasters turn my stomach."

"They sure do!" Mary-Kate giggled. "One time Ashley ate two corn dogs before riding a coaster and—"

"Spare me the details!" Kristen groaned.

Ashley stood up. She was about to head for the magazine rack, when she caught Mary-Kate reaching behind Colton's chair—and slipping a green envelope into the pocket of Colton's sweater!

Ashley recognized the envelope. It was from Mary-Kate's set of Christmas cards.

But when Ashley looked closer, she saw a tiny sticker. It showed a pair of smiling lips along with the word SWAK.

Ashley knew what SWAK meant. It meant Sealed With A Kiss. It also meant something else. . . .

She was sure Mary-Kate was making a big mistake!

CHAPTER THIRTEEN

"Are you sure Ms. Keech is asleep?" Mary-Kate asked. It was after lights-out and the girls had met on the main floor as planned.

"Positive," Cheryl said. "Ms. Keech may sound chirpy, but she snores like a jackhammer."

Ashley could feel her heart pounding in her chest. Sneaking down to the tunnels was scary enough. But they could get into big trouble sneaking around after lights-out!

"Let's get this over with," Ashley pleaded.

Quietly the girls made their way through the storage room and down to the tunnel.

"Rats!" Mary-Kate muttered.

"Where?" Ashley gasped, looking around.

Mary-Kate shook a flashlight she had found in the utility closet. "The battery in this thing is wimping out."

The girls walked until they found the door they were looking for. Ashley held her breath as Mary-Kate pulled the doorknob. She pulled several times before giving up.

"That's funny," Mary-Kate said. "The door wasn't locked this morning."

"Great!" Ashley exclaimed. She quickly switched her smile to a frown. "I mean—oh, great. Now we'll have to go all the way back to our rooms."

"Wait!" Mary-Kate said. She pointed to a narrow tunnel. "I know we never went through this one."

"Let's not and say we did," Ashley blurted out.

"But we're down here already," Mary-Kate said. "We might as well check it out."

The tunnel led to another staircase. After climbing it, the girls found themselves in front of a door.

"Now where are we?" Ashley asked.

Mary-Kate shone her weak flashlight around the room. Everyone gasped as the beam landed on Ms. Keech's portrait of Mr. Turnbull.

"It's Turnbull's office!" Mary-Kate exclaimed.

Ashley's knees turned into jelly. If Turnbull found them—they'd be history!

"Are we sure it's Turnbull's office?" Cheryl asked.

"It's got to be," Mary-Kate said. She reached for a picture on the desk. "Look. Here's a picture of Mr. Turnbull and . . . and . . . "

"And who?" Ashley asked.

Mary-Kate gulped. "And Colton!"

CHAPTER FOURTEEN

"No way!" Ashley cried. She glanced over Mary-Kate's shoulder and gasped. "Oh, no—it *is* Colton!"

Mary-Kate eyed the picture. Colton was wearing a neat polo shirt and shorts. Mr. Turnbull was wearing a neat polo shirt, shorts, and a barbecue apron that read WHO INVITED ALL THESE TACKY PEOPLE?

"Check it out," Cheryl said. "Those two are practically clones."

Mary-Kate felt Ashley shake her arm. "That's who Colton really is," Ashley told Mary-Kate. "He's Mr. Turnbull's son!"

Mary-Kate stared at her sister. That made no sense at all!

"Son?" Mary-Kate laughed. "Are you crazy?"

"Actually," Elise said, "Colton never told us his last name. And those stories about his family are far out."

"No wonder Colton stuck up for Mr. Turnbull," Kristen said. "He was defending his dad."

Mary-Kate's head was spinning. She had heard enough!

"What was that noise?" Mary-Kate said. "It sounds like someone's right outside the office."

In a flash, everyone bolted out the back door.

Mary-Kate wasn't sure she heard anything. She just knew that she wanted to get away from that picture!

"Attention, boys and girls," Mr. Turnbull announced in the dining hall Friday morning. "There will be no grilled cheese sandwiches for lunch today. Instead, there will be cabbage soup and sardine sandwiches!"

Mary-Kate could hear Elise and Cheryl gag. And she could feel Ashley staring at her.

"You didn't sleep much last night, did you, Mary-Kate?" Ashley asked.

"Why do you say that?" Mary-Kate asked.

"You have circles under your eyes," Ashley pointed out. "And you don't even realize you're pouring ketchup on your waffles."

"Huh?" Mary-Kate's hand froze around the ketchup bottle. Then she forced a smile. "It's an acquired taste."

But Mary-Kate knew Ashley was right. She hardly slept a wink last night. She was too busy wondering about Colton.

"I guess we'll never find out what's behind that other door now," Cheryl said, pouring another glass of juice.

"Why not?" Mary-Kate asked.

"Because I am not going back down to those tunnels," Cheryl declared. "I'm tired of sneaking around."

"Me, too," Kristen agreed.

"We have to go back," Elise said in a small voice.

Everyone turned to look at Elise.

"I dropped my Peppermint Pink blush in the tunnel," she explained. "It must have fallen out of my sweatshirt pocket last night."

"Why can't you just buy another one?" Kristen asked.

"Because," Elise said. "Peppermint Pink was discontinued last month."

Ashley took a deep breath. "Do you remember where you dropped it?" she asked.

"Probably in front of that locked door," Elise said.

"That's when I pulled a tissue out of my pocket. I can't imagine life without my Peppermint Pink blush!" she wailed.

"Okay, okay," Ashley said. "We'll go down after breakfast. We'll find the blush. Then we'll leave."

Mary-Kate nodded with the others. But her stomach was doing cartwheels. If they found Colton—maybe they could find out the truth!

CHAPTER FIFTEEN

After breakfast, Mary-Kate, Ashley, Elise, and Cheryl met in the storage room.

"Where's Kristen?" Mary-Kate asked.

"She said she had a sore throat," Elise said. "So she stayed in her room to gargle."

"Okay," Mary-Kate said. She pointed the flashlight at the door leading to the tunnel. "Let's roll."

The girls hurried through the tunnel. Elise found her blush right where she thought she'd dropped it.

"Got it!" Elise said happily as she reached for the compact. But as she was about to pick it up, a pounding noise filled the tunnel.

"Footsteps," Ashley exclaimed. "Someone's coming this way!"

"It sounds like they're coming from Wesley House," Cheryl pointed out.

"It's Mr. Turnbull!" Ashley shrieked. "Colton told him we were here. And now he's coming for us!"

Ashley let out another shriek as a shadowy figure appeared around the corner. Then another. And another.

Mary-Kate aimed her flashlight at the shadows. Then she narrowed her eyes and frowned.

"It's the boys!" Mary-Kate declared. "And Kristen!"

Ashley stared at Kristen. "I thought you had a sore throat," she said.

"Gargling does wonders," Kristen replied.

"So does blabbing," Ashley snapped. "You said you wouldn't tell the boys about the tunnel."

Kristen pulled Mary-Kate and Ashley aside.

"I know I said I wouldn't blab," Kristen said. "But that was before I got to know Garth."

"Garth?" Ashley cried.

"Yeah," Kristen whispered. "I never knew brains could be so irresistible!"

The boys looked up and down the tunnel.

"This is excellent!" Garth said. "Just like the ancient Roman catacombs."

"Or that cool new computer game," Derek said. "Loopy Labyrinths!"

Victor nodded. "Or that new spy video—"

"Don't get too cozy," Ashley interrupted. "We were just about to leave."

"Not us!" Garth said. "Kristen told us about some secret locked door down here. And we want to check it out."

"There it is!" Kristen said, pointing to the door.

The last thing Ashley wanted to do was open that door. Who knew what was behind it?

"It's locked," Ashley pointed out. "You can't open it without a key."

"That's what you think," Tyrone said. He and Garth backed up—and threw themselves against the door.

BAM! The boys staggered back.

"Once more!" Tyrone gasped.

This time the door flew open.

"Another staircase." Cheryl peered up the steps.

"And whatever it leads to," Ashley said, "Colton doesn't want us to find it."

"Which is exactly why we should check it out!" Mary-Kate said.

"Are you serious?" Ashley cried.

"Sure," Mary-Kate said. "Maybe the answer to the picture we found is right upstairs."

"How excellent!" Tyrone cried. He rubbed his

hands together. "I feel just like Indiana Jones!"

"I feel like James Bond!" Victor declared.

Tyrone smiled. "I feel like—"

"Let's just do it already," Mary-Kate interrupted. By the beam of Mary-Kate's flashlight, the kids made their way up the stairs.

That's funny, Ashley thought. *This staircase is different from the others. It has a carpet!*

Mary-Kate opened the door at the top of the stairs. But this time they didn't find themselves in a classroom, a kitchen, or a library.

They found themselves inside a fancy ballroom!

"Wow!" Ashley gasped.

A crystal chandelier hung from the ceiling. Velvet wallpaper and oil paintings in gold frames covered the walls. A thick red carpet was on the floor. And in front of a stained glass window stood a tall Christmas tree with tiny white lights.

"This has got to be the Harrington mansion," Ashley said.

"How did we end up inside the Harrington mansion?" Mary-Kate asked.

Ashley heard a rustling sound. She spun around and saw the Christmas tree shaking back and forth.

"Whoa!" a voice shouted from behind the tree.

Ashley and the others stepped back. Falling out

from behind the Christmas tree—was Colton!

Colton landed on the carpet with a thud. His glasses were crooked on his face, and his usually neat hair was messed up.

"What are you doing here?" Mary-Kate asked.

"Master Colton!" a voice interrupted. "Your pizza muffins are ready."

Everyone turned. Ashley saw a tall man dressed in a black suit standing at the double doors.

"Busted." Colton sighed under his breath.

"Master . . . Colton?" Ashley repeated.

"Thanks, Higgins," Colton told the man. "I'll be there in a few minutes."

"Very well, sir," the man said as he stiffly left the room. "I'll keep the muffins warm."

Ashley glanced at Mary-Kate. Her sister looked just as confused and surprised as she was.

"Ballroom? Butler?" Cheryl asked. She planted her hands on her hips. "Can someone fill us in here?"

Colton sighed. "I didn't want you to find out."

"Find out what?" Mary-Kate asked.

Colton took a deep breath. "That I'm a Harrington," he replied. "Colton Harrington III!"

CHAPTER SIXTEEN

"Colton Harrington III?" Mary-Kate cried. "But your parents were charged by rhinos. You said so yourself."

"That was just a story," Colton admitted. "I'm really a direct descendant of Phineas T. Harrington III."

Mary-Kate's head was spinning. Now things were really getting weird.

"If you are a Harrington," Mary-Kate said, "then how come we never saw you before?"

"Because I go to boarding school in Switzerland all year," Colton explained.

Mary-Kate's heart sank. Ashley was right all along. Colton was not who he said he was.

"Why did you lie to us?" Mary-Kate asked.

Colton stared down at his shiny shoes. "My mom and dad went to Rome for the holidays," he said. "And this time they couldn't take me."

"What does that have to do with it?" Mary-Kate asked.

"Being alone during the holidays is the pits," Colton explained. "So when I met you girls, I thought I'd finally have some fun."

"In those dusty, smelly tunnels?" Ashley asked.

"Those tunnels were my secret hideaway for years," Colton said. "My private place to hang."

"But why didn't you just tell us you were a Harrington?" Mary-Kate wanted to know.

"And have you guys think I was a snob?" Colton asked. "That's what you all call us Harringtons, isn't it?"

Silence.

"That's why I came up with all those stories," Colton explained. "And kept you from going up the stairs to my house."

Mary-Kate watched as Colton paced the room. She was mad at Colton for lying, but she felt sorry for him, too. It probably wasn't easy feeling different.

"It's okay, Colton," Mary-Kate said with a smile. "I think it's cool that you're a Harrington."

"Yeah," Ashley laughed. She looked at the other girls. "And at least you're not—Son of Turnbull!"

"Son of who?" Colton asked, confused.

"We found a picture of you and Mr. Turnbull," Cheryl explained. "What was that all about?"

"Oh, that!" Colton laughed. "That was taken at the Harrington family barbecue last July. Turnbull likes people to think he's tight with us Harringtons."

Mary-Kate breathed a sigh of relief. So that explained it!

"So you don't think I'm a rich snob?" Colton asked.

Mary-Kate looked around the lavish ballroom. "Rich, yes," she said. "Snob, no."

The double doors to the ballroom swung open. Higgins walked in again. "Master Colton, a guest has arrived," he said.

"Who?" Colton asked.

"A Mr. Charles Turnbull," Higgins announced.

Everyone gasped.

"Now we're really toast," Mary-Kate groaned.

But when Mr. Turnbull entered the ballroom he had a big smile on his face. And a goofy Santa hat on his head.

"Greetings, kids!" Mr. Turnbull said. "I was just

going to ask Colton if we could use his ballroom for a big holiday shindig!"

The kids stared at Mr. Turnbull.

"Why the stares?" Mr. Turnbull asked. "Do I have pizza muffin in my teeth?"

"No!" Ashley said. "It's just that you're acting so . . . you know . . . different."

"You can thank Sylvia—I mean Ms. Keech for that," Mr. Turnbull said. "She made me realize that life is too short to be grumpy—especially around the holidays."

"But you were grumpy!" Mary-Kate said bravely. "And lately you've been acting kind of—"

"Weird?" Mr. Turnbull interrupted with a grin. "It was all an act so the party would be an even bigger surprise. That was Ms. Keech's idea, too."

Mary-Kate smiled at Ashley. The pieces were all falling into place!

"So what will it be, Colton?" Mr. Turnbull asked. "Can we use your ballroom to 'party hearty,' as you kids say?"

"Bring it on!" Colton said with a smile.

Everyone high-fived. But when Mary-Kate looked at Colton, she felt a pang of sadness.

Suddenly everything had changed.

*　　　*　　　*

"This party rocks!" Ashley cheered on Saturday night. "And it beats washing dishes at the soup kitchen."

"That's tomorrow," Mary-Kate reminded Ashley.

It was Christmas Eve. The kids from all the forms were in the Harrington ballroom wearing their best clothes and dancing to a deejay. Even Mr. Turnbull and Ms. Keech were twisting on the dance floor.

"Good thing I packed my velvet dress," Ashley told Mary-Kate.

"Good thing you packed two velvet dresses," Mary-Kate said with a smile.

Tyrone, Derek, and Victor walked over. They were wearing goofy Christmas pins on their jackets.

"Excellent party!" Tyrone said. He pulled a string on his Rudolph the Red-nosed Reindeer pin and the nose lit up.

"Where's Garth?" Mary-Kate asked.

Derek pointed to the dance floor. Garth and Kristen were slow-dancing—to a fast Christmas song by Alvin and the Chipmunks.

"He'll get over it." Derek sighed. "Come on, guys. Let's get some of that awesome fruitcake."

Ashley laughed as the boys pushed their way through the crowd. "I guess they are kind of cute," she said. "In a geeky way."

Mary-Kate nodded. But her eyes were searching the ballroom for Colton. She saw him talking with the deejay.

"Go for it, Mary-Kate," Ashley said.

"What?" Mary-Kate asked.

"Ask Colton to dance," Ashley said. "You have my approval, you know. Now that he finally got real."

"Thanks," Mary-Kate said. "But I had a better chance with Colton when he was a tunnel rat."

"What do you mean?" Ashley asked.

"Face it, Ashley," Mary-Kate said. "He's a Harrington. Why would Colton Harrington III want me when he can date any girl on campus?"

"Why don't you ask him?" Ashley said. She pointed over Mary-Kate's shoulder.

Mary-Kate spun around. Colton was coming her way!

"I think I'll try some of that fruitcake," Ashley said with a gleam in her eye. "See you!"

The closer Colton got, the more Mary-Kate's stomach fluttered.

"Hey," Colton said.

"Cool party!" Mary-Kate began to babble. "I really like the Christmas tree. And the decorations. And the wreath on the door with the fake snow—"

Colton reached into his pocket. He pulled out a

familiar green envelope. "And I really liked your card," he said with a grin. "Especially the sticker on the back."

Mary-Kate smiled when she remembered the Sealed With A Kiss sticker. "You know what they say," she said with a shrug. "'Tis the season to get real."

"'Tis the season for something else," Colton said. He pointed to the ceiling.

"What?" Mary-Kate asked. She looked up and saw mistletoe hanging from the ceiling. And when she looked back down—Colton surprised her with a kiss!

Mary-Kate stared at Colton for what seemed like ages. Then she smiled and said, "Want to dance?"

"Sure," Colton said.

The deejay played a slow song by 4-You. As they danced, Mary-Kate looked over Colton's shoulder and gave Ashley a wink.

Her sister was right after all.

There was more to Colton than they could have ever imagined!

Happy holidays!

HO, HO, HARRINGTON!

by Elise Van Hook

The students who stayed at Harrington over winter break were in for a surprise treat!

Mr. Turnbull, everybody's new favorite Grinch-turned-Santa, provided the goodies for a huge holiday party at the Harrington mansion. And our new friend, Colton Harrington III, provided the ballroom!

Everyone dressed their best and danced the night away under a cherub chandelier. There were decorations galore—not to mention lots of food! The crowd chowed down on pizza muffins and fruit-cake.

For dessert there was eggnog for some . . . and

kisses under the mistletoe for others. But that's a whole other article. . . .

GLAM GAB
THAT'S A WRAP!
by Ashley Burke
and Phoebe Cahill

Fashion expert Ashley Burke

Fashion rules at holiday time—and we don't mean just velvet dresses and sequined bags! Your presents need a little dressing up, too! Here are some really cool ways to decorate your gifts this season:

• Is your wrapping paper a little too plain? Well, it doesn't have to stay that way! Cut holiday shapes out of construction paper and paste them onto the package. You can also use stickers, crayons, or glitter to make your present look extra-special.

• Hang an ornament on your friend's package and watch her eyes light up! Some great choices are

candy canes, holly, glass balls, pine cones, and foil-wrapped Santa chocolates.

• Presents don't just come in boxes anymore! Transform baskets and even Christmas towels into the perfect gift wrap. Gift bags are great for all those really small presents. Don't forget to toss in a little red and green confetti!

SNOWBOARD 101
by Mary-Kate Burke

Sports pro Mary-Kate Burke

Okay, guys—get ready for a lesson in my new favorite winter sport—snowboarding! I'm sure you all know the basics. First put on snowboots and attach them to your snowboard. Then position yourself at the top of a snow-covered mountain—and fly (or fall) all the way down!

But here are a few cool facts about snowboarding that you might not know.

Snowboarding started in the 1960s. Some dude who liked skiing and surfing decided to put the two together, and *bam!* The snowboard was born.

There are three kinds of snowboarding techniques. Alpine is when you slalom down a hill. Freestyle is when you do tricks with the board. Boardercross is a mix of the two. I haven't mastered any of these techniques yet—but I did manage to get to the bottom of a hill once without falling down!

THE GET-REAL GIRL

Dear Get-Real Girl:
My best friend is a boy. We used to hang out together

all the time. But now he has a girlfriend. And I'm jealous! He's spending way more time with her than he does with me! What should I do?

Signed,
Lonely Girl

Dear Lonely:
Hmm. Are you sure your buddy is "just a friend"? It sounds like you have something more romantic in mind. Maybe you should examine your feelings more closely. If friendship is what you really want, let him know how much you miss your

time together. But if you want him to be something more—well, you're on your own!

Signed,
Get-Real Girl

Dear Get-Real Girl:
I have tons of schoolwork, tons of after-school activi-

ties, tons of events . . . and tons of stress! I don't want to give up anything I'm doing but it's getting to be too much! How do I deal?

Signed,
Overworked

Dear Overworked:
Deeeeeep breath. It sounds like you've got a lot on your plate! What you need to do is organize your life. Make yourself a schedule so you can fit in everything you want to do. But

don't forget to schedule in some free time!

Signed,
Get-Real Girl

THE FIRST FORM BUZZ
by Dana Woletsky

It's freezing outside! So grab some hot chocolate, wrap yourself in a big blanket, and get ready for some White Oak/Harrington gossip that's hot enough to melt a glacier!

Who was MKB kissing under the mistletoe at the

holiday party? Sources tell me it's a new Harrington hottie—from a very old Harrington family!

Speaking of kissing, is it true that KL's latest crush is more into computer games than into smooching? In that case,

this may not be a match made in holiday heaven.

Talk about nightmares! CM woke her roomie up four times this week—

reciting elephant jokes in her sleep!

And next time I go see a scary movie, remind me not to ask AB to come along. I heard that this first-former couldn't take the heat down in the Harrington tunnels. She was scared of everything!

Found—one tube of glitter blush on the steps of the Harrington mansion. Could it possibly belong to EH?

That's all for now folks. Remember, if you want the scoop, you just gotta snoop!

UPCOMING CALENDAR

New Year's Day may be January 1st, but here at White Oak we're celebrating it again and again! Come to the belated New Year's party being held in the Student Union this Saturday, January 5.

You won't believe your eyes! Harrington will once again amaze you at the

annual magic show on February 24th. But tickets to the event are disappearing fast—so hurry to the ticket office in Hampton Hall to buy yours today!

Valentine's Day is just around the corner, and hearts everywhere are a-flutter! Want to show your sweetie how much you care? Put a special valentine in the *Acorn*. Entries must be in by next week.

Will the groundhog see his shadow this year? Join us to find out! The time: 8 A.M. The place: the ground-

hog's very humble abode! (Otherwise known as the hole in front of Phipps House.)

Come in from the cold! Porter House is having a cocoa party this Friday night.

IT'S ALL IN THE STARS
Fall/Winter Horoscopes

Scorpio
(October 24-November 22)

You have a tough decision to make this month, Scorpio. But if there's one thing that the Scorpion knows, it's how to tell the difference between wrong and right—in any situation. Go with your instincts and you won't be sorry!

Sagittarius
(November 23-December 21)

As an Archer, you're quick and impulsive, and you like to get things done. Sometimes you're so busy you can hardly slow down! Don't forget to take a little time for yourself. Lounge on the couch, watch lots of movies, and eat ice cream out of the carton. You deserve a break!

Capricorn
(December 22-January 20)

Goats always get where they want to go, no matter how rocky the climb. Now's the time to use your discipline and determination to help your friends reach their goals, too. With a loyal Cap at their side, the sky's the limit!

PSST! Take a sneak peek
at

#21

Now You See Him, Now You Don't

"Come on, Ross!" Ashley said. "We only have two weeks to learn this trick before the magic show."

Ashley sighed. She and Ross were in the auditorium practicing for the annual Harrington magic show. Ross was supposed to put Ashley in a box and cut her in half. But so far, she was still in one piece!

"I'm doing the best I can." Ross frowned. "Maybe if you got in the box the way I told you to, we wouldn't have a problem."

"Maybe if you gave me better instructions I would know what I'm doing," Ashley shot back.

She and Ross glared at each other.

"Why don't I just practice by myself for a while," Ashley said. She folded her arms.

Ross shrugged. "Fine," he said. "I'll be sitting in the first row of seats if you need me." He jumped off the stage.

Ashley glanced out at the darkened auditorium. She and Ross were the only ones left at practice. Everyone else had left an hour ago.

She climbed into the box and pulled the lid shut. Then, as quickly as she could, she lowered herself into the secret compartment.

Yes! she thought. *I did it!*

"Hey, Ross!" Ashley said. "I got in really fast that time! Did you see?"

No response.

"Ross?" Ashley called. She turned her head. No one was in the auditorium.

Ross had left her all alone!

"Ross, where are you?" Ashley cried. She banged on the top of the box. But the lid was locked tight.

She was trapped!

Oh great, Ashley thought. *What do I do now?*

"Ross Lambert!" Ashley yelled. "I'm going to get you for this!"

Here's an excerpt from our newest
Mary-Kate & Ashley series

so little time

#1 HOW TO TRAIN A BOY

Chloe carefully rearranged her position on the edge of the trailer steps, stretching out one leg and leaning back on her elbows. Maybe the movement of her bright pink top would catch Travis Morgan's eye.

She sneaked another look.

Travis was still concentrating on his stupid dirt bike.

Okay, this isn't working, Chloe thought. She needed another plan. She walked over to her puppy, Pepper, and gave her a pat.

That's it! Chloe thought. She'd try to train Pepper with the dog obedience book her father had bought. Travis would notice and come over to talk. After all, who could resist a puppy?

Chloe picked up the book from the steps and

began to read. "'Eye contact,'" she read. "'Establish dominance by getting your dog to blink first.'"

Chloe read a few more pages, then decided to try out a couple of commands. She untied Pepper and walked a few steps away. The puppy started to follow.

Chloe turned to face the dog. "Stay," she commanded. She held her palm out, put a stern expression on her face, and stared the dog in the eye. "Stay."

Pepper stopped walking.

"Whoa, I don't believe it," Chloe said. "Good dog!"

Next, Chloe went over to Pepper and pushed down on her rear end. "Sit," she said. The dog sat, then stood up again. "Sit," Chloe repeated, still maintaining eye contact.

Pepper plopped down on the deck.

"Good dog!" Chloe grinned and petted her. "Okay Pepper, speak!" she commanded.

The puppy kept quiet, but a nearby voice said "Hi."

Chloe spun around.

Travis Morgan was sitting by his dirt bike, gazing at her.

Chloe stared back, totally surprised. Then she glanced at the dog-training book in her hand. No way, she thought. No way this book could work on a boy . . . could it?